Wake Up, Wilson Street

Library of Congress Cataloging-in-Publication Data / Thomas, Abigail.   Wake up, Wilson Street / by Abigail Thomas; illustrated by William Low.
Summary: A young boy and his grandmother get up very early and watch the morning activity in their neighborhood. ISBN 0-8050-2006-3
[1. Morning—Fiction.   2. Grandmothers—Fiction.]   I. Low, William, ill.   II. Title.   PZ7.T364Wak   1993   [E]—dc20   92-10873
Printed in the United States of America on acid-free paper. ∞   First edition   10 9 8 7 6 5 4 3 2 1

For my family, love and thanks
—A. T.

For you, Peggy Low, with love
—William

Henry Holt and Company ✧ New York

Wake Up, Wilson Street

Abigail Thomas ✦ Illustrated by William Low

Lots of people live on Wilson Street but Nana and Little Joe are always the first ones up. "You're an early bird," says Nana, "just like me."

"Shhh," says Nana as they tiptoe down the stairs. "Mommy and Daddy are still asleep."

"Shhh," says little Joe. They are quiet as mice.

Nana makes two cups of cocoa and little Joe puts a marshmallow in each cup.
"Yum-yum," says Nana. "Yum-yum," says little Joe.

They sit in the big rocker and look out the kitchen window. Little Joe is snuggly in Nana's lap.

"Wake up, Wilson Street!" says Nana. But it is still dark.

One, two, three, four, five birds on the telephone wire. The sky is getting lighter.

Here comes Charlie the paperboy on his bicycle. He wears a red hat. He has newspapers in his basket, and he throws one against the front door, *whomp!*

"We'll leave it there," says Nana. "We're not in a hurry."

Mrs. Kopeck is the next person up. She opens her front door and bends down for her paper. Then she looks at the sky. It is going to be a fine Saturday.

She sees Nana and little Joe in the window and she waves. They wave back. Then Mrs. Kopeck starts to sweep her front porch. "She likes to get a jump on the day," says Nana.

Next Mr. Oakley comes out of his house. Everybody calls him the Duck Man. He is carrying a big paper sack. Nana and little Joe look down the street.

This morning there are ten ducks waddling along the sidewalk to Mr. Oakley's house.
He feeds them every morning. "Quack-quack," say the ducks.
   "Quack-quack," say Nana and little Joe. "Quack-quack."

Down the street Nana sees the shade go up on the window of Mr. Vernell's grocery store. Next the door opens and Mr. Vernell carries a big basket of tomatoes outside.

Then he carries out a big basket of corn. "Corn," says Nana. "Mmmmmm."
"Mmmmmm," says little Joe.

A milk truck stops in front of the grocery store. The driver carries a big tray filled with milk bottles into the store. "My," says Nana, "that looks heavy." The truck drives away.

"Brrrrm," says little Joe.
"Brrrrm," says Nana.

"Look!" says Nana, pointing out the window. "Two squirrels!"
"Look!" says little Joe.
Next door, Mrs. Gregory comes outside with her easel and her paints.

She is making a picture of her house, which is white with red shutters and a red chimney. Mrs. Gregory always wears a straw hat. Mrs. Kopeck walks across the street to have a look.

"An artist needs to catch the morning light," says Nana.

Now Mr. Morris comes outside with a bucket of soapy water and two sponges. He is going to wash his car before it gets too hot. The sun is getting higher in the sky. Victoria is going to help her father. He gives her a blue sponge to dip in the bucket. She likes to see her face in the clean hubcap.

"What a funny mirror!" says Nana.

Now Nana and little Joe hear noises coming from upstairs.

Here comes Mommy in her pink bathrobe. "Good morning," says Mommy, and she gives little Joe a kiss. "Have you two had your breakfasts yet?"

"Not yet," says Nana, and little Joe shakes his head. "We've been much too busy."

Finally Daddy comes downstairs. He is always the last one up on a Saturday morning. His face smells like shaving cream and he kisses little Joe.

"Good morning, everybody," says Daddy, and he yawns a big yawn. "My, we're all up early today!"

Nana and little Joe look at each other but don't say a word. They know they're the *real* early birds!